Albert Samah

WEEPING ENVIRONMENT

(Short Stories)

Miraclaire Publishing
Kansas City / Yaounde

MIRACLAIRE PUBLISHING LLC
Kansas City, (MO) USA

Email: info@miraclairepublishing.com
Website: www.miraclairepublishing.com

P.O. Box 8616 Yaounde 14,
Yaounde, Cameroon

ISBN-13: 978-0615707853
ISBN-10: 0615707858

Copyright © 2012 Miraclaire Publishing LLC
Albert Samah

Disclaimer
Miraclaire Publishing makes every effort to ensure the accuracy of all the information ("Content") in its publications. However, Miraclaire and its agents and licensors make no representations or warranties whatsoever as to the accuracy, completeness, or suitability for any purpose of the Content and disclaim all such representations and warranties, whether expressed or implied to the maximum extent permitted by law. Any views expressed in this publication are the views of the authors and are not necessarily the views of Miraclaire.

To My Lord Jesus Christ who by coming into my life brought meaning and to all friends and lovers of nature

ACKNOWLEDGEMENTS

For proof-reading and insightful contribution, thank you Nnam-Mbi Dzenyagha, Godlove Eghombi, Irene Ntabe, Francis Yong, Denis Chenwi, Belinda Chouh, Yvonne Eghombi for all you did.

For Moral and Material Support: Thank you Kingsley Musong, Rev. Alfred Njini, Rev. Paul Kebafa, Vitalis Asanji, Holy Asanji, Gipson Mundah and friends at Madison Park Limbe.

For company and friendship; thank you Elvis Eghombi, Bliss Eghombi, Priestly Eghombi, and Royalty Eghombi.

For counseling and mentoring, heartfelt gratitude to Bernadette Tchakoani and Hilarion Wirdzeka Faison of the Ministry of Arts and Culture, Yaounde and Prof. Wilfred Mbacham of the University of Yaounde 1, Cameroon. For a great and understanding family: the Samahs of Tiben Village.

Contents

Story One

Global Climatic Warnings

Once upon a time, Mr. Forest, Miss Sea, Mr. Ozone, Mr. Plant, Miss Earth Surface, Mr. Wildlife, Mr. Lake, Miss Atmosphere and members of the natural environment lived with Humankind in harmony as one big family. They both depended on each other for survival. But as time went on, Humankind increased greatly in population on the surface of the planet earth. This increase exerted a lot of pressure and demands on the natural environment. To make matters worse, Humankind engaged in a sophisticated and extravagant lifestyle that exhausted the resources of the ecosystem. This was becoming increasingly unbearable to the natural environment. This led to suspicion and mistrust between humankind and the natural surroundings.

It was as a result of this that Natural Environment decided to convene the All Natural Environment General Assembly. This meeting was to be attended by representatives of plants, animals, birds and the natural world. The topic of discussion was to be the abusive use of Natural Environment by Humankind. The deliberations were tense and it took three weeks for a consensus to be reached. After this general assembly, it was decided that the permanent and non permanent members of the Security Council of the Natural

Environment takes a firm decision on what to do. In another extra-ordinary session, members were asked to plead their case so as to avoid any legal lapses. They were to make sure their complaints fell within the framework of international norms and Natural or Universal law. The first to raise his case was Mr. Wildlife also nicknamed Endangered Species:
"Your Excellencies," he said,
"I thank you all for this opportunity to address this extra-ordinary session of our kind, the Natural World. I am called Endangered Species because I am fast becoming the last of my kind on this entire planet earth. I have seen first class wickedness from the human race. Humankind has indiscriminately killed my kind for reasons I cannot tell. We had pleaded with Humankind to stop killing our young ones. We said even if they must kill, we the fathers and mothers were prepared to give up our lives for our children; so that for our today they can see their tomorrow.

Humankind has rather increased the rate at which they kill our progeny. I, therefore, on behalf of all my kind, and to honour the lives of those of my kind that Humankind has killed, place in my vote for serious action to be taken against them. Justice must be done. Blood for blood! Progeny for progeny! Yes capital punishment for Humankind. I rest my case."

Albert Samah

It was then the turn of Mr. Forest to speak. He stood up, arranged the microphones placed on the rostrum and began:

"I am not only a witness of the injustices and abuses of Humankind, but also a living victim. We have been destroyed indiscriminately in our numbers by villagers for firewood. We are being cut down and sometimes for very silly reasons. When Mankind wants to build houses they cut us down. When they want to farm, they cut us down. Sometimes when they want to hunt, they cut us down. Ladies and gentlemen, brothers and sisters, in this struggle eh! eh! eh! Worst of all, selfish logging companies destroy us in rates that cannot be measured. If you really want to know the rate at which we are being destroyed on a daily basis, just take a walk beside any seaport in Central and West Africa. You will see for yourselves the number of us being dragged overseas. Sometimes, this genocide carried out against us is done in complicity with their so called national governments. Even though Humankind knows that it takes about two hundred years for some of our kind to grow to maturity, they keep destroying us. Sometimes, in the process of destroying the old, they also destroy the newborns. Where will our legacy be when we are gone? Will our legacies be found just in houses, tables, cupboards, papers? I ask for justice to be done according to international norms and Universal Laws and standards. Capital punishment for humankind and his progeny."

Miss Earth Surface took the floor immediately Mr. Forest finished;
"Ladies and gentlemen," he said, "There is nothing Humankind can do without me. Just like there is nothing he can do without any one of us. But there is nothing Humankind has not done to afflict us seated here and those

we are representing. Humankind keeps destroying my fertility, nutrients and beauty. Not only am I over farmed, but even the way I am being farmed destroys me daily. I am farmed in such a way that when Mr. Rain is passing (without any bad intention on his part), he carries part of me down to the seas. This destroys my strength, nutrients and beauty. Ladies and gentlemen each day I die in the inside." There was murmuring in the room as the other members of the earth Security Council looked at one another and shook their heads.

"I am not through," Miss Earth Surface continued.

"They would not stop destroying me in the process of farming. They burn me up with the pretext that in some parts of the earth, I am not fertile. They say the need more yields. The height of their wickedness is when they pour toxic chemicals in the name of trying to fertilize me. Oh I tell you my friends in this suffering, it's painful! Do you know that in the process of farming Mr. Forest they also inflict me with pain? What should I say more? Is it the overgrazing carried out on me? I can go on and on but I will stop here. I also call for judgment according to international law and Universal custom" When Miss Earth Surface finished her presentation, there was a standing ovation.

In her presentations, Miss. Sea, representing all water bodies like streams, rivers, lakes and wetlands also complained that she had been suffering from toxic waste. She said toxic waste from industries was dumped into her, on a daily basis and in large quantities. She said spills from natural oil companies were also deposited into her. This was the cause of the loss of aquatic life. She also complained of over exploitation and abuses carried out against some members of her family by human kind. She spoke of a huge decline of marine fisheries because human beings use all kinds of nets

Albert Samah

to catch fishes of all ages. She also called for serious sanctions to be taken against mankind.

It was the turn of Mr. Ozone. But his speech took a different turn:
"Ladies and gentlemen," he said, "I would not belabour the points already made. The human race is incomprehensive in its relationship with us. That we all know. I will just present a few instances where I have been offended. On daily basis, Humankind keeps sending all kinds of emissions to destroy my body. Chlorofluorocarbons from old refrigerators, those used by fire extinguishers, those from air conditioners and plastic forms have also been killing me softly. But I think that we should not take any harsh decision against human kind." There was murmuring in the room. The representatives turned and whispered to each other.

"I am not yet through ladies and gentlemen. I think International Natural Justice is already taking its course against Humankind. Right now as I speak, harmful ultraviolet rays transcend me to reach mankind. I am no longer a shield for the sun's rays. Do you want to know the consequences? Skin cancer and…. So let's allow International Natural Justice to take its place."

The presentation of Mr. Ozone was followed by that of other members of the Security Council, especially the non permanent member. Amongst them was that of Miss Atmosphere. In her presentation, she complained that she has been suffering suffocation from fuel and gasoline consumed by cars. She also said that the suffocation came from the discharge of sulfur and nitrogen oxide from power plants that burned coal for electricity. She said the activities of industries polluted her in ways that no one could understand. She complained that worst of all industrialization was on the increase.

After all the presentations had been made, there was a break. The session was due to continue after sixty years. This was quality time given for mankind to act. During this time, a lot of negotiation went on among the different members of the Security Council on the decisions to be taken on the issues on the ground. Some members of the Security Council especially those with veto rights had personal interest as a result of their secret dealings with Humankind. The fear amongst some members of the Natural Environment was that some members of the Natural Environment with veto rights might prevent any serious sanction to be taken against the human family.

When Humankind heard of this meeting, some members of his family began organizing conferences on environmental protection. These meetings were to combat any sanction or reaction from Natural Environment. These meetings took place in different parts of the world. The first took place in Stockholm in Sweden. But there was disagreement between the major groups of the human race.

"We must put all our resources together to see that we meet some members of the natural environment to stop their actions against our kind. I think if we work secretly with some of the members who have veto rights, we can know the plans the Natural Environment is putting against us. We can even bribe some of them so that they use their veto rights to stop any sanction against the human family as a whole," the Developed countries proposed.

"We cannot be talking about fighting against Natural Environment when we are living in abject poverty. You go ahead and do whatever you think is good," the Developing countries said.

Albert Samah

"But their action is and is going to affect us all. We cannot do it all alone even if we want to. No member of the Natural Environment will accept a deal that other members of Humankind are not committed to," the Developed countries argued.

"Yes, but you don't have any real problems like we do. Our present priority and commitment for our people is development and not environmental protection," the Developing Nations on their part argued.

There was no concrete decision arrived at during this meeting. However, it created awareness on the problem on the ground. As much time was wasted on the decision to be taken, some members of the Natural Environment family were already taking sanctions against humankind on their own accord.

In 1986 in Norway, the human family organized another meeting concerning the threats of the Natural Environment Family. It was called the Brunthland Meeting. During this meeting, human beings pledged to engage in the kind of development that will be beneficiary to the present and the future generation; that is, thinking on the future and welfare of its offspring. It was followed by another in 1993. In the one that took place in Kyoto in 1997, there was a sharp suspicion between members of the group of the Developed countries. Personal and economic interest was placed above that of the entire human kind. In another meeting that followed, the sharp disagreement that existed between the Developed and the Developing countries emerged.

"But you should fix it. You are more responsible for the complaints Natural Environment is accusing our kind of," the Developing countries said.

"You cannot say we are the only ones responsible," the Developed Countries quarreled back.

"You are. Look at what you did: The Industrial Revolution. Look at your extravagant lifestyles."

"What about your poor farming methods, the burning down of trees for wood and all …I think this is not time for arguments. This problem is going to affect us all. There is no time to waste. When Natural Environment attacks, it is going to affect us all. The attacks from Natural Environment will not take into consideration who attacked or abused her." Then turning to their right, the Developed Countries said, "If Natural Environment attacks, you will suffer more because you do not have the means to protect yourself against such attacks or even to adapt."

So, it was that as Humankind argued on, the Natural Environment decided to meet. Though in the outset there was disagreement on the types of sanction to be meted on Humankind, they finally agreed that they were to give some sanctions as a first warning to Humankind. If Humankind refused to comply and seek for peace, they were to look for other means. This operation was to be led by Climate Change with the help of other members of the Natural Environment. It was dubbed *Operation Global Warming*. Natural Environment was to begin by causing the environment to get hotter and hotter on the surface of the earth. This would make the entire globe to get warmer. This was going to cause failure in food production and consequently bring famine to some members of Humankind. Climate change was going to cause the ice in the North Pole of the earth surface to start melting so that the sea levels would rise and cause floods and if possible destroy human settlements. When Climate change began the operation, the effects were immediately felt on planet earth by all Humankind.

It was based on this that Humankind decided to seek peace

Albert Samah

with Natural Environment. They pleaded guilty to all the allegations. They accepted to pay huge reparations and made commitments to stop the indiscriminate and over exploitation of Natural Environment. Humankind promised to plant more trees as reparation for those they had destroyed in Mr. Forest's family. They also said they would look for other sources of energy like solar energy.

Mankind further pledged to stop the indiscriminate killing of Mr. Wildlife's family especially his children and those members of his family that were already facing extinction. With Sea, they agreed to stop destroying aquatic life by treating the types of material poured into streams, rivers, lakes, wetlands and seas. They also said they were to stop the use of nets that caught young fishes.

With Miss Soil, they agreed that they would stop overgrazing and watch the way they cultivated her. They promised to recycle any material that could prove dangerous for her livelihood. They also promised Mr. Atmosphere that they would stop pollution by treating the kind of gases that went to the air. They said they would use other sources of energy like biogas so that the rate of emission would be reduced. They agreed that they were to see into it that each human person reduced his or her carbon print, that is, every human person would reduce the amount of energy used. It was said that those who had cars were to decide to trek on some days. It was decided that children would be educated on how to reduce the consumption in their homes. They were to always turn off the lights, television, computers and other electrical appliances after use.

Their pledge to Mr. Ozone was that old refrigerators be destroyed so that there should be less emission of Chlorofluorocarbons. When all these promises and commitments had been made, Natural Environment agreed to make peace with humanity. Natural Environment however said that if mankind did not hold on to these commitments, she was to increase the sanctions by intensifying the operation; the operation which was launched at 0.5 degree would be increased to 2.00 degree centigrade. Natural Environment also said that if Humankind continued treating any member of the Natural Environment poorly, Humankind and their descendants will be sanctioned accordingly.

Story Two

*W*ildlife Fellowship

*B*efore weapons were ever manufactured, mankind and animals lived happily in their different worlds. With time, mankind started manufacturing weapons for self defense and to attack animals. Mankind began by fabricating ordinary weapons like slings, cutlasses, spears, bows and arrow and many other simple weapons. As knowledge increased, mankind created more sophisticated weapons like pistols, Kalashnikov and other kinds of guns. With these new types of weapons the activities of mankind increasingly interfered in the animal kingdom. The discovery of the locally made gun in Cameroon called *Cha'avum* used for hunting led to the killing of numerous animals. This led to untold pain and misery amongst the animals.

But there was division amongst human beings as to the treatment given to animals. A section of mankind started a movement on the rights and welfare of animals. This section constructed wildlife centres where animals that were arbitrarily arrested and who suffered aggression could seek refuge. These wild life centres were referred to by animals as either Animal Asylum Centres or Animal Embassies. Amongst the numerous Animal Asylum Centres in the world, Cameroon had three located in different regions: One in the South West Region called the Limbe Wildlife Centre. The second found in the Centre Region, called the Mvog Betsi zoo and the third of these Animal Embassies located in the South Region.

As hunting and the destruction of the forest which serve as home for several animals kept increasing, some animals escaped to these Animal Embassies. Animals who succeeded to get into these Animal Embassies counted themselves fortunate and privileged. One day as the animals of the Limbe Wildlife Centre went about their daily activities, one of the animals remarked,

"Life without efforts can sometimes be very boring"

"What do you mean? We have all what we need here. What else on earth do you want? Leopard asked.

"Do you know that we have more food and protection than many human beings in the world? What are you saying?" Zebra asked.

"We do not have to be ungrateful. Let's not be like some human beings who do not know how to be thankful," Preuss Monkey commented.

"You do not understand. What I mean is that some potential in us cannot be discovered simply because we do nothing on our own. Being here, it's difficult for us to try

Albert Samah

new things. It is in the process of trying new things that we get into self discovery." Chimpanzee said.

"Are they also some human beings like us who just sit, eat and play? I think man is a very busy creature," Preuss Monkey added

"Ha! Ha! Ha! Never mind some of these human beings. They are busy bodies. Some of them you see passing here in the name of going to work are very lazy. When they get to work, they start sleeping or playing computer games. Some of them are a lazy set of creatures," Lion said.

"I am already feeling bored in this place. Just sitting, eating and playing. I do not want to be like one of those human beings," Zebra complained.

"I have an idea. I think we should get to know each other better. We should introduce ourselves, share our experiences and get to know each other better," Antelope suggested.

"That is a great idea. I think we can start straight away," Chimpanzee agreed happily.

"I think it will not be very serious if we start today. We shall start tomorrow. We should take one person a day. In this way we shall get to know one another in a very personal and intimate way. This is how it will go; we shall each give names and surnames and our maiden names if there are any. After self introduction, we shall recount the circumstances and how we got to this Animal Embassy called Limbe Wildlife Centre. We shall also let one another know our likes, dislikes and our aspiration for our individual lives and family and for the entire animal family. Bring along your laughing teeth because there will be much to laugh about."

So, the following day the animals began the exercise. The first to begin was Preuss Monkey:

"Ladies and gentlemen of this great animal kingdom,

14

I count it a privilege to start this exercise which I think is going to bring us a lot of fun. I want to thank you my dear brother Antelope for bringing such a brilliant idea. Without taking much of your time, I will begin. My name is Preuss Monkey. I am also called Cercopithecus Preussi (human beings say this is my scientific name) I have been termed endangered because the enemy has killed almost all of my kind. I came from the Rain forest around the Cross River of the Savannah River. Some of my family members are found around Mount Cameroon.

In families like ours we are usually between 6-18 members. The oldest male member in our family is equally the family head. Members of my family are predominantly introverts. That is, we are usually quiet. As concerns our hobbies, we like living on the ground. I think that is all I can say about myself for now," When Preuss Monkey said the last word, there were reactions from here and there.

"You have not even started my friend. What are your favourite meals?" Donkey asked.

"Oh my friend Donkey, I know that is the only thing you were going to ask. You and food are just like... let me not say it. O.K my favourite meals are leaves shoots, fruits, lichen, fungi and sometime insects."

"OK the circumstances that brought you into this animal embassy," Donkey pointed out. Preuss Monkey hesitated for sometime before he continued.

"It is a story that I do not always like to share because even though I made it here, my experience was never the best. It happened that one day an enemy came into our home in North Cameroon. Our leader had summoned us and we were about having our evening discussion, when suddenly one of my elder brothers shouted "Enemy! Enemy! Enemy" Before we knew it, we heard gun shots in the air. It got one of my brothers but he succeeded to escape with the bullet in his body. All of my family members succeeded to

Albert Samah

escape.

I was the youngest. I was barely 6 months old. I tried to escape but could not make it. I saw my brother, sisters, father and mother for the last time. When the Enemy caught me, he took me straight to his house. He constructed a little house for me. His plan was that he would sell me.

One day, some good people saw me and reported to the Green Officers. They were the ones who brought me here," Preuss Monkey explained.

By the time Preuss finished, tears had gathered in his eyes. One of his kind came and hugged him and gave him a leaf which he had plucked from one of the pear trees which Preuss used as a handkerchief.

"Take it easy, brother, take it easy. It shall be well with us Monkeys, whether human beings like it or not," another Monkey consoled and prophesied.

The second animal to do her presentation was Chimpanzee;

Thanks for giving me this time to introduce myself to you and to share some information on who I am. My presentation will be two fold; First I will tell you what I know about myself and secondly what Mankind says about me. I share all this with pleasure and humility. I am called Chimpanzee. We were once a great species, found in twenty five countries in the world. But right now we are found in only four countries in the world, one of which is Cameroon. According to mankind, I am the closest relative to human beings and share 98% of his genes. They say we are the most intelligent animal. That is what Mankind says. It's good I make this precision. We communicate with our brothers and sisters through many gestures. We also use facial expression and body gestures. I think these are some of the reasons why mankind says we are closest to him. We love to spend time on tree tops and on the ground. We do a lot of drumming.

"Yes, tell us how you came here. Others will also have to speak, Camel cut in.

"Don't tell me you are already jealous of Chimpanzee. Jealousy is a human thing. It's not part of us animals. Go on Chimpanzee," Tiger said.

"I was almost about giving my testimony on how I came here. It happened that some enemies visited our home. They came with sophisticated weapons and killed everyone in my family. They were about to kill me when one of them said they should take me to Douala to sell. On their way to Douala, I was praying in my heart that God should intervene and save me from the hands of those wicked men. We passed through several checkpoints but none of the Police officers saw me. At one point I tried to shout but they held my mouth. At one of the check points, a policeman discovered me but the enemies gave him 5000 Francs and they allowed them to pass through the checkpoint with me. But I kept praying. As we left Tiko and were about entering Douala, some Forest officers (the Green Men) saw them and suspected them of something illegal. They asked them to open their bags. When they did, I quickly jumped out. It was this Forest Officer who took me and brought me here"

After the presentation of Chimpanzee many other animals did their presentations. The last days of the presentation were the most exciting. Some animals that were not there when the exercise began had joined. Even some human beings came to eavesdrop. But something strange happened. While one of the animals was doing its presentation, two men walked into the wild Life Centre. As they approached the area where the animals were having fun, the animals started whispering to one another. Then one after another the animals started leaving. At one point, one of the animals shouted "Enemies". The animals started running in confusion. There was great confusion. To the surprise of both the animals and the men, Chimpanzee and Preuss Monkey just sat where they were.

As the men approached, Chimpanzee and Preuss Monkey discovered that the men were some "unauthorized" hunters who had sneaked into the centre. They had come to the centre to frighten these animals. They wanted to make these animals to live in perpetual fear. In that way the animals would not enjoy their peaceful stay in the centre. When they got to where these animals were, one of them asked,
      "Are you not also running like you friends?"
      "Did I hear you say run?" Chimpanzee asked.
      "Yes, R.U.N" The one who asked the question spelled the word as he answered.
      "Why should we R.U.N?" Preuss Monkey asked.
Then looking around to see if there was anybody around, one of the men said,
      "We are of the most sophisticated and deadly hunters that Animal kingdom has ever known" When Chimpanzee and Preuss Monkey heard, they clapped their hands and laughed. By this time the other animals where watching from afar.
      "We are one of the most sophisticated and deadly hunters that the animal kingdom has ever known," Chimpanzee and Preuss Monkey jointly mimicked.
      "Listen whoever you think you are, we are not ignorant of who we are. We are "totally protected". We are "endangered species", we know our rights," Chimpanzee said.
      "Yes we know our rights. There is nothing you can do against us because of our numerical inferiority. And if

ever you do anything against any one of us, I mean those found here as well as those who are in the forest; you might spend the rest of your miserable lives in prison. We know the national and international laws protecting us. If you do not know, I advise you to find out," Preuss Money said. With this, the men did not say a word. Then suddenly all of the animals started clapping and shouting.

After that incident, the animals continued with their presentations. When the presentations were through, the animals wrote down everything that was discussed and every participant signed. They also wrote down some of their aspirations and wishes. This was attached to the presentations. Both were sent alongside a letter to the Minster of Forestry and Wildlife.

In the letter, they thanked the government, other Non Governmental Organizations and donor stakeholders for the efforts they had made to keep them in the various centres in Cameroon. They also thanked all well wishers especially those citizens who intervened and brought some of them to the centre. To these citizens, they said their kindness will be forever written boldly in the Animal chronicles.

They requested that the government and other stakeholders should reinforce their efforts in protecting their brothers and sisters who are still living vulnerably in Cameroon and other parts of the world. They also called on these stakeholders to propose animal friendly programmes in schools so that future generations of mankind will grow up to love and protect them. They further requested that those interested in the welfare of animals should engage in tree planting exercises so that animals would have confortable places to live in.

Albert Samah

In concluding their letter, they expressed their desire to live in places that resemble their original habitat. They also said they would like to visit some forests to enjoy their habitats. They expressed their wish to exchange visits with animals of other wildlife centres in Cameroon and Africa so that they could share experiences.

The End

Story Three

The Friendship Vows

Once upon a time Mount Cameroon and Limbe Sea were very good friends. Their friendship had existed for several centuries before mankind ever thought of settling at the foot of the mountain and beside the seashores. Though they lived several metres apart, they always communicated with each other. They supported one another and relied on one another for strength. While Mount Cameroon protected Limbe Sea from the harshness of the sun rays, Limbe Sea on her part gave Mount Cameroon a solid foundation to stand and assert itself like one of the tallest mountains in Africa. Whenever the height of Mount Cameroon was to be measured, the count always started from the sea.

Albert Samah

As time went on, mankind decided to start visiting both the sea shores of Limbe and Mount Cameroon. However, human beings paid more visits to the seashores than to the mountain top. Some human beings even decided to settle by the seashores. This is because the top of Mount Cameroon is very rough and cold. The few people who visited Mount Cameroon were some villagers who went to the mountain for hunting. Human activities carried out around Mount Cameroon and especially around Limbe sea shores became harmful to the calm relationship that had existed between these old friends for centuries.

Mount Cameroon could no longer hear the gentle waves from the sea that hit the rocks and Limbe Sea could not also enjoy the calmness of the mountain as a result of human activities like hunting and sightseeing. The Mount Cameroon Race which brings people from different parts of the world to compete yearly also sometimes preoccupied the mountain. As a result, there was absence of communication between these aged-old friends. This did not only strain their relationship but brought about competition, jealousy, envy, bitterness, strife and gossip. It was in this light that Mount Cameroon decided to discuss the issue with another friend called Menchum Falls.

"Ever since mankind began visiting and settling around Limbe Sea, my relationship with Limbe Sea has never been the same" Mount Cameroon said.

"I have realized that," Replied Menchum Fall

"You see, self-sufficiency and pride can be very dangerous. It is the worst of vices both to nature and human beings." Mount Cameroon continued.

"Have you ever tried to discuss this issue with her?" Menchum Fall asked.

"Limbe Sea is very proud. She thinks he does not need us now. Before mankind came we have lived together as one big family. She grew in fame by my hands. Was it not just of recent, that is in 1841, that Alfred Saker crossed over and gave her the name of the Queen of England, Victoria? The name which was later changed to Limbe? Before then, Hanno, the Carthaginian had seen my might long ago, reason why he gave me the title, *Chariots of the gods*. That was when he saw me from afar demonstrating my might. I was shaking my body and spitting out fire with loud shouts like those of a warrior. Human beings call it eruption," Mount Cameroon recalled.

"I think we should have an All Nature or Natural Environment meeting (General Assembly)," Menchum Fall suggested.

"Yes if we keep discussing this issue just the two of us, someone might take it down to Limbe Sea and she might put it in her own way" Mount Cameroon remarked.

"It is not as if we do not want human beings especially foreigners to visit Limbe Seas. We equally want Limbe to help mankind if need be. Our worry is that we are a family just like the human race is a family. So the activities of the human race should not tear apart the unity that exist amongst us the Natural Environment family. You see how united the human race is against us," Menchum Fall commented.

"My friend Menchum Fall, let's not get there, do you really think the human race is united? When there is ethnicity, religious conflicts between the Christians and the Muslims, class struggle between the poor and the rich, racial segregation between blacks and white, gender discrimination between male and female, generational gap struggle between the young and the old? As a matter of fact the list that characterizes division among humans is a long one. My friend let's set a date for the General Assembly of the Natural Environment," Mount Cameroon said.

Albert Samah

It was from this discussion that a date was set for Mount Cameroon, Limbe Sea, Menchum Fall and the Wind to meet. Wind was commissioned to inform Limbe Sea of the date and the time of the meeting. The agenda of the meeting was clearly spelled out: "Human activities hindering our unity." Unfortunately, Wind who was to carry the information on the date of the meeting was eavesdropping on the conversation between Mount Cameroon and Menchum Falls. He used the piece of information he heard to increase the suspicion and misunderstanding that had been going on between Mount Cameroon and Limbe Sea.

"Do you know Mount Cameroon and Menchum Falls are planning to eliminate you?" He told Limbe Sea.

"Why will they be thinking of such impossibility? I am too big to be swallowed up by a Fall or a Mountain. Not even Climate Change or Global Warming in all their power and pride can think of this impossible thing" Limbe Sea replied calmly.

"But why do they keep saying you are too ambitious, proud and arrogant?" Wind asked.

"I think they have every reason to say so. Look at the number of people who visit me in a year. Look at the number of people who have constructed houses, hotels and parks beside me. Look at the number of people who depend on me for food because of my fertility and the protein I provide to the people through fish. Think about the transportation I provide to people of different countries. People traveling to and from Nigeria and Cameroon make use of me. It is equally the same with people traveling to and from Cameroon and Equatorial Guinea. Do they know the quantity of crude oil I give mankind? Are these not enough reasons for them to be jealous and say I am proud and arrogant?" Limbe Sea asked.

"I think you are right. My advice to you is that you should not attend the General Assembly of the Natural

Environment," Wind cautioned.

"Why? I must. I don't think my progress means someone's failure," Limbe Sea said.

"It is my modest advice. Mount Cameroon can be very malicious and vicious." Wind said as he took his leave. But before the beginning of the meeting, Wind, who nobody ever knows when and where is coming or where is going but for experienced weather forecasters, met with Menchum Fall and Mount Cameroon separately.

"You haven't heard the latest news in town" The Wind declared as he clapped his hands and sat down on a tree beside Menchum Fall. Cutting down the branches of this tree.

"What latest news? Weather forecast. So where will you be going this time to cause havoc? At least you should have alerted me that you were coming. Mechum Fall sighed and said.

"First hand information from Limbe Sea. He said he can at least appreciate Mount Cameroon for its touristic importance. He said of what use are you to mankind? He said months in, months out, year in, year out you keep making the same useless noise, *jug, jug, jug, jug, jug-jug-jug*…" Wind said.

"Stop it! Stop it! Stop it!" What did you just say? Menchum Fall asked as it reduced its noise. "It is just because human beings in Cameroon had deliberately refused to generate electricity from my strength I should have been producing energy that will generate electricity to all of the Central Africa and even beyond". Menchum Falls said.

"By the way Limbe Sea said he and human kind are too busy preparing for the construction of a seaport. He said he does not have time to attend meetings with people who do not progress" Wind said as he took his leave.

Immediately he left, Menchum Falls he went to see Mount

Cameroon. When he got to Mount Cameroon, he continued with the same gossip and lies telling. He told Mount Cameroon that Limbe Sea said he should be contented in keeping the few endangered species that are still remaining on the Mountain rather than organizing unprofitable meetings. Wind told Mount Cameroon that Limbe Sea said because he is not productive he wants to gain strength from others by organizing all sorts of useless meetings. He said the only thing Mount Cameroon is known for is that it is called one of the tallest mountains in Africa with just a height of about 4100 metres. He also said this title does not put food on the table for human beings especially Cameroonians. Wind said Limbe Sea acknowledged that from time to time Mount Cameroon shakes his buttocks and cause some destruction to mankind. When Wind finished his narration, Mount Cameroon as usual was calm and silent.

"Don't you have anything to say Mount Cameroon?" Wind asked.

"Yes, Limbe Sea is right. How have I been helpful to human kind? I do not provide roads for mankind to get to the other parts of the world like Limbe Sea does. Even mankind especially the Bakweri people have been complaining that I simply occupy space that should have been used for the construction of good roads, schools and stadia among other infrastructure," Mount Cameroon replied.

"How could they say that? Is it not because of you that one of their kindred, Sarah Etonge of no great academic or social status is known over the world? She has won the first prize of the Mount Cameroon race in the female category several times. She is not alone. Think of other Cameroonians like Lekunze Timothy, Ngwaya Yvonne and many other Cameroonians who have been known internationally as a result of you, the mountain race," Wind pretended to console.

"How could they say that?" Turning to himself

Mount Cameroon said, "If only mankind knows the hidden treasures that are found within me". And if only Limbe Sea could realize that as human beings depend on her so much on protein, they will soon deplete her of some of her resources like fisheries. They will also destroy her through pollution.

"But that is not enough reason for Limbe Sea to utter all those stupid words against you." Wind said.

"Even if Limbe Sea refuses to attend the meeting there will be no problem"

Wind left Mount Cameroon discouraged because of the calm and light hearted manner in which Mount Cameroon spoke. To him it simply meant that Mount Cameroon can still and will look for other ways to resolve the misunderstanding that exist between him and Limbe Sea. Then as fast and unsettled as the Wind is, he left immediately and told Limbe Sea, that Mount Cameroon said he should prepare for war. With this Limbe Sea started roaring and foaming, mobilizing its strength to leave its shores and move up to meet Mount Cameroon.

Meanwhile, Mount Cameroon on his part was groaning with anger on what Wind said. He however had pretended as though he was not offended when Wind said those words. Without letting the Wind nor Menchum Fall and Limbe Sea to know his plans, Mount Cameroon carried out a surprise attack on Limbe Sea and the inhabitants leaving beside Limbe Sea. Lava came out of the mouth of Mount Cameroon and descended towards Limbe Sea. It destroyed food crops and palm trees. It began heading towards some human settlements like Semme Beach Hotel and Madison Park found around the Limbe seashores. The Mount was furious and everywhere her anger was demonstrated by smoke and explosions of all kinds. When Mount Cameroon's attack got to Bakingili, human beings who had settled around Limbe

Albert Samah

Sea began pleading with Mount Cameroon to stop her attacks. Though still very furious, their cries soften her heart and she decided to stop the attack. When she did, Limbe Sea then decided to dialogue with Mount Cameroon. It was then that they both realized that Wind had been feeding them with wrong information. They then decided that as part of one big family, they would do everything to live in peace with one another. They also promised to help mankind for as they said mankind is also part of a bigger family with Natural Environment called the ecosystem. On the day when the peace deal was signed in Bakingili, Menchum Falls wrote and sang this song for Limbe Sea and Mount Cameroon:

Below the banks of Bakingili
Just besides the gentle hills
Where God asked the seas to stop
Lies the inheritance of Mount Cameroon's anger

Passersby of all tribes and tongues
Now stop to wonder and ask
What the mountain ate so much, that it
Vomited angrily and buried these innocent trees

If only they knew this little story
That once upon a time,
Mount Cameroon went to visit an angry old friend
The Limbe seashores, the beauty of God's handiwork

When Limbe Sea and Mount Cameroon listened to the song they both clapped and laughed over it.

The End

Weeping Environment

Story Four

*D*eath Has No Favourites

*T*hings that happen to others are indicators of what could happen to us. There was a man called Mr. I -know-All-Things. He was so terrified of death. He said he had not yet enjoyed life to its fullest and was not prepared to die. Every day when he was about to sleep, he would tell his wife and children that he was practising on how to die. He once told his wife that if he went to practise how to die (for this was how he called sleep) and that if he did not finally come back she should know that he had practiced enough on how to die and that he was qualified to play, eat, dance and sleep with death.

One day, Mr. I-Know-All-Things told death that whenever

Albert Samah

he was prepared to come for him, he should inform him and not come for him as a surprise. He complained bitterly that it was usually the habit of Mr. Death to take people by surprise.

"You walk beside people; you hide inside accidents, abortions, diseases, just waiting for the least opportunity to take them away. But I have one request to make to you: Mr. Death, whenever you decide to come and take me, inform me, so that I may make peace with my neighbours and pay my debts. In that case, my creditors will not trouble my wife and children. Also, I have to go to church and confess my sins so that I will meet with God as friend and not as enemy. Mr. Death agreed and accepted to inform Mr. I Know-All-Things whenever he was prepared to come for him.

Three weeks later, one of Mr. I-Know-All-Things neighbours died. Everybody was surprised because the deceased person was a young man of about 36 and had been healthy and strong until that morning when he complained of light headache.

That evening when he died, several of his neighbours, friends and relatives gathered to condole and share their sympathy with the man's wife and children. They gathered in groups in his compound. Mr. I-Know-All-things was discussing in one of those little groups and he said,
        "It was this morning that I talked with him, when I got out of bed. We even had to meet this evening so that we could see the *chef du Quartier* to arrange for the clean-up campaign in our neighbourhood. But now he is dead and gone. No illness, just like that. Death is very troublesome."

The following Thursday, exactly six days after his neighbour's death, Mr. I-Know-All-Things received news that his cousin who was in the United States had just passed

Weeping Environment

away some few hours ago. He was perplexed. It was not only the untimely death that caused the confusion and the pain, but also the fact that this cousin had just left Cameroon some months earlier and much had been invested in his departure. While receiving his friends and colleagues who came to condole with him, Mr. I-Know- All-Things said:
"Death has surprised us again, Mr. Death has surprised my family and my cousin."

Five days later, when Mr. I-Know-All-Things returned from the village for the burial of his cousin, he went straight to report to his boss that he was back. He wanted to use the opportunity to ask for leave since he had other things to do before he could fully resume work. When he got to the office, he saw a notice with the picture of his friend and colleague with whom he shared the same office. He did not want to believe it when he read through the announcement. It said his colleague died in a car accident when he was traveling to his village. Mr. I-Know-All-Things cried and wailed at the top of his voice. His colleague was his best friend and was to him like a brother. They shared the same office and even their problems. Mr. I-Know-All-Things had even proposed that his first son would get married to his colleague's daughter.

Three days after this incident, Mr. Death decided to visit Mr. I-Know-All–Things. He fell ill and was taken to hospital.
The doctor said he had malaria, and that it was at a critical stage. Mr. I-Know-All –things started feeling strange. He felt as if he would never recover from that illness. He went into a trance, and then he saw how his wife and children were weeping and wailing. He saw how the priest was officiating at his funeral ceremony. He saw some of his family members fighting over his property. Some wanted his wife, others wanted his car while others his bank account. But no one

wanted to take responsibility for his children.

"What is happening to me? This cannot happen to me now!" Then he heard a voice that said, "I am Mr. Death." Mr. I- Know-All-Things got up and said;

"You cannot do that. You said you would keep your promise. You promised to inform me before coming. Now you are coming to take me without any notice."

"You are to blame, I informed you not once, not twice but on several occasions. I came right into your neighbourhood and took away your neighbour just to inform you that I would be coming, but you never wanted to listen. Then I came to one of your family members, telling you again that I was on my way but you failed to listen. I thought by passing through your friend and colleague you would at least understand and prepare, but you deliberately refused to listen." Mr. Death then continued. "Now tell me who is to blame."

Mr. I-Know- All-Things bowed down and said. "I am sorry I never knew you were speaking to me. I failed to realise it. Give me another chance," Mr. I-Know –All-Things replied panicking.

"Because you were conscious of me and asked me to inform you whenever I was to come, I am giving you another chance. Be prepared for me at anytime."

Mr. I-Know-All-Things recovered from the malaria. He went back home and made peace with everybody. He did everything he was supposed to do in his office, in his family and in his community. He advised his friends that one ought to live each day as if he were to die the next day. That is, by not doing the things that one would be afraid of, if one had to die the next minute and by doing that which one is supposed to, if he or she were to die the next minute.

He said whatever thing one has to do, he or she should do it immediately and does it well because death can visit us at anytime.

He also said whether poor or rich, literate or illiterate, strong or weak, black or white, employed or unemployed, death has no favourites.

The End

Story Five

The Divided Kingdom

Many years ago all the diseases lived in perfect
harmony as one big family. As a result of their unity, they
were strong and were a great danger to the human race.
Nothing mankind did could ever defeat them. Their unity
prevented mankind from discovering their secrets and
weaknesses. As time went on, mankind became very
conscious of Malaria and of Humano Immuno Virus -
Acquired Immune Deficiency Syndrome often called to
simply as HIV/AIDS. As much attention was paid to them
they became very popular especially amongst humans.
Everywhere amongst human beings, the biggest story was on
what HIV/AIDS and Malaria were doing. This aroused
jealousy in some of the other diseases. One of those who

were very worried by the increased fame of Malaria and HIV/AIDS was Syphilis.

One day he said to himself, "Why is it that every day one hears only of Malaria and HIV? Do they want to prove that they are superior to all of us in this kingdom?" From then on, he conceived a plan to put these two diseases against each other and to sow hatred between them. He believed that by doing so, their fame would reduce. He decided to pay a visit to Malaria, fully prepared to launch his wicked scheme. As he approached Malaria's residence, he heard Malaria singing happily. "What must have made Malaria this happy?"He asked himself. Immediately a thought came to him and he conceived a plan to quench this happiness. When he knocked at the door, Malaria was lost in singing.

> Malaria is a very great guy
> Malaria is a great great guy
> Malaria is a great great guy
> You must be careful lest I kill

Syphilis was surprised that though he had been standing there for three minutes, Malaria was still busy praising himself. In his song, he sang how he had been causing destruction amongst human beings. He sang of how he changed the name of the African continent. Africa was referred to as the Whitman's grave because of his activities. He sang on how he had been the cause of the death of great missionaries and explorers who came to Africa. It was when Syphilis faked a cough that Malaria turned and realised that there was somebody standing behind him.

"Oh my good old friend; how has it been? It's been quite some time," Malaria said smiling.

"It's been long, as you can see, and this is because you no longer visit me. By the way, why are you so happy?"

Albert Samah

Syphilis asked. Malaria then went ahead to recount his successes and achievements to Syphilis.

"I am so happy because I have been and I am still classified as one of the greatest destroyers amongst human beings."

"I can see. But it surprises me that each time when I meet with HIV and AIDS, he says he is the greatest in our kingdom and that even the human race has classified him so. He told me that each day, you become more jealous and feel threatened by him because he has gradually taken your place and you can no longer hold the title of *pichichi* of death. He said that because of this, each time you meet with him, you are so furious and bitter towards him." These words acted on Malaria like a sword that had been pierced into the heart of a soldier on a battlefield. Syphilis had succeeded to sow a seed of discord amongst these diseases who had always been good friends.

The following day, when Syphilis visited HIV/AIDS he equally found him very happy and singing.

> The first shall be the last
> And the last shall be the first
> The first comes last and the last comes first
> Aids came last but is now is first,
> You must abstain lest I kill

When Syphilis knocked, he did not wait for any invitation to get in. He immediately went into the house.

"What is making you this happy?" Syphilis asked. "When I heard your voice it was so beautiful that I thought some angels just descended from heaven." He continued while stretching his hand to pick a seat to make himself comfortable.

"I sing whenever I sit back and evaluate my

Weeping Environment

achievements in the kingdom of human beings," HIV/AIDS replied proudly.

When Syphilis asked what his achievements were, HIV/AIDS went on to recount all the troubles he had brought to the human race. He said though he was born just in 1983, he had been able to accomplish much for the kingdom of diseases. He said his hard work had made him to be known and dreaded amongst human beings. He said they talked about him on the radio, television, in schools, in hospitals and even in churches. When he finished recounting his fame, Syphilis remarked, "You must be a very great guy. What has been your secret?" HIV laughed and nodded. He boasted of all the things he had done to achieve success in his activities.

He went ahead to reply that in schools he had succeeded and still continued to succeed when pupils and students get involved in sexual immorality, especially on school benches, in abandoned buildings and in their dormitories. In offices, he said, he succeeds when some bosses go as far as having ungodly sexual relationships with their secretaries. While in the homes of some native doctors, and in some hospitals, it was and is because some of them use unsterilised objects. When he finished narrating, releasing and unveiling his secrets, Syphilis remarked,

"You must be a great person. And I see no reason why Malaria says you   eak as a vegetable and that without him you can't succeed." These words fell on HIV like a deep knife. It was to him as painful as the news of the death of a loved one. Not only did it destroy HIV`s excitement on his achievements but it also poisoned his mind towards Malaria.

Two days later, Malaria decided to pay a visit to HIV/AIDS and to find out why HIV had to destroy the love and unity

Albert Samah

that existed in the kingdom of diseases. On his way he decided to stop at Cancer's residence. On arrival, he met with HIV/ AIDS. Without any friendly or formal greeting, he launched his accusations against HIV/AIDS.

"So who do you think you are, HIV? Why have you been spreading false information that I am as weak as a vegetable and that without you I wouldn't have been able to succeed?" "Wasn't it you who told Syphilis that I am a nobody?" HIV replied furiously

"But are you not one?" Malaria said as they now faced each other quite ready to exchange blows.

"Are you not just being jealous because as young as I am, I have gradually taken away your position in this kingdom?" HIV and AIDS said walking around with his hands in his pockets.

"What position are you talking about? If all the young men decide to abstain from pre-marital sex, if all couples decide to be faithful to their partners and if all the doctors and nurses and those in barbing studios decide to sterilise their objects before using them, where then will you have the strength to withstand the human race? As for me, I have been since time immemorial strong and dreaded by mankind" Malaria said nodding his head and raising up his shoulders.

HIV clapped, laughed and said, "You see mankind is already through with you. If only mankind knew that keeping their houses and bodies clean could wipe you away in a second. If only they listened to the advice of the doctors then you could have been long buried. Anyway, I hear mosquito nets are available everywhere so then you are half dead if every human being starts using them as effectively as prescribed in hospitals. I can already see tears streaming down your eyes."

At this point, Cancer stood up to stop the quarrel that was almost turning into a fight.

"Let's not fight amongst ourselves for we are a family and a kingdom. A kingdom that is divided cannot stand against a common enemy. HIV, you must control your anger and you Malaria learn to keep your mouth shut"

"Who made you a supervisor over us?" HIV/AIDS asked.

"What have you achieved against humanity that you think you can be a leader over us?" And before he finished speaking, Malaria stepped in this time against cancer.

"Listen Cancer, you have no reason to tell me to shut my mouth because even in the kingdom of diseases we have the freedom to express ourselves." Looking at them, Cancer sighed and left. He was so disappointed by their reaction towards him. The others also took his example and followed suit without a solution found to resolve the dispute. On the other hand, it proved to be an advantage to mankind, for they came to know much about HIV/AIDS and Malaria and the rest of the diseases. This was how mankind came to know the causes of these diseases and brought out solutions on how to conquer them.

The End

Albert Samah

Story Six

Cholera must be Defeated.

Mbanwei Primus got several names from his classmates and peers because despite the hard work with his studies he had repeated the General Certificate of Education (G.C.E) Ordinary Level five times. Some called him "the reader who never read enough". Others referred to him as the "unfortunate John Book." Still some simply nicknamed him "The ever faithful G.C.E client"

When Mbanwei failed the G.C.E for the first time, his parents were really concerned about it because they knew how committed their son was to his studies. Immediately schools resumed that academic year, they came to discuss with the Academic Master concerning the issue. Having discussed lengthily with the Academic Master of City Bilingual College, they left satisfied that things would be positive the following academic year. That year, unlike many students who usually write the G.C.E for the second time, Mbanwei redoubled his efforts. "I must make it," He told himself time and again. He increased his reading hours almost at the expense of his health.

But when the National Station of the Cameroon Radio and Television began reading names of successful candidates for that year, Mbanwei's name was not amongst. It was in one of those years where complete results for both successful and unsuccessful candidates were read. When it got to City Bilingual College, it was read out that Mbanwei had just two papers. He wept for two good weeks and refused to be comforted even by the principal who happened to live in the same neighbourhood.

When he failed the G.C.E for the third time, Mr. Ndogho and his wife decided that something had to be done. They heeded the advice of some of their friends who said their son had certainly been bewitched and that they should go back home for cleansing. Others still advised them to see one of the *mallams from* the North of the country, or the *babas* from Oku who according to them were great experts at divining and rendering solutions. To fight for their son's future, Mr. Ndogho travelled home to Mamfe for sacrifices to the gods of their ancestors before proceeding to Oku through Batibo and Bamenda. That year, the G.C.E results were released earlier than expected. But the results were not a respecter of ancestors or *babas* so Mbanwei failed.

For the fourth time, Mbanwei had to sit for the same examination. This time his parents brought in several home teachers to assist him. They also fought spiritually. Through their contact holy water was given by one Parish Priest for Mbanwei to sprinkle on his face each time before reading. A litter of anointing oil was got from a newly arrived

Albert Samah

Pentecostal Pastor. Mbanwei had to anoint his books and pens before using them. Nonetheless, he did not make it that year.

But neither Mr. Ndogho nor his wife nor Mbanwei himself gave up. They knew that something was wrong somewhere but they could not lay their fingers on. They knew that if they held on they would certainly learn from where the problem ensued and with this they would be able to help others in the future.

As was the tradition of City Bilingual College, twice every year there was a come together for the parents, the teachers and the students. This was usually under the auspices of the Parents Teacher's Association (P.T.A). This meeting was usually to discuss academic matters. Mme Ntabe Nnambi was asked to give a talk on preparing and writing exams effectively. It was believed that through such talks, parents might be able to identify some of the difficulties that their children faced both in school and at home.

When Mme Ntabe Nnambi took the floor, she explained that many students failed both the G.C.E Ordinary and Advanced Level not because they did not study well but because of negligence and failure to obey basic instructions. To illustrate her point clearly she narrated a little story that happened in one primary school in Bamenda. She said, Mr. Mbong wanted to test his pupils' knowledge on Cholera so he began by asking the pupils some questions on Cholera.

"What is Cholera?" He asked.
"I sir! I sir! I sir!" The pupils scrambled to answer so as to receive the reward of a "well done" and "clap for him" or "clap for her."
Mr. Mbong began by pointing at Mosima to answer the question. Mosima got up and began,

"One day, Auntie Babara ate *achu* and *yellow soup* which had cholera because the water which they used in making *achu* and the yellow was from the well and the well was not treated. So she started passing out much water. By the time she was taken to hospital, she had lost much water. So that is how Auntie Barbara died because of that wicked cholera."

Mr. Mbong simply nodded his head and proceeded to another. This time around she pointed to Nkolo. She stood up, arranged her gown and began explaining.
"My mother said that we should never buy *folere or yaourt* by the roadside because we do not know the source of the water which was used to make them. She also said that we should make sure that we wash our hands with soap every time we come back from school, church or from visiting our friends." Again. Mr. Mbong nodded, excused himself and went out where he could laugh aloud with out frustrating the pupils. When he came back, he pointed to Paul who said,
"When uncle Tom came back from Haiti, he told us that it was one Whiteman from.... em em ...I think Brazil who brought cholera and kept it in Haiti. So, after the earthquake in Haiti, cholera began spreading because there were dead bodies everywhere and water got contaminated. He said cholera came from there."

Before Paul could ever finish, Michael had cut in and said,
"Paul wants everybody to know that he has an uncle who is in Haiti." When Mr. Mbong got it, he scolded at him and asked Michael to answer the question. Michael stood up and said,
"Our auntie Susan in the Sunday school told us that the devil is a bad devil and the devil is a liar. She said cholera came from the devil. But in the name of Jesus, cholera must be defeated."

Albert Samah

Before Mme Ntabe Nnambi could ever finish the story the hall had exploded into laughter with tears coming out from the eyes of some of the parents, teachers and students as well.

Then she continued with the educative talk. "This is exactly what happens with some of our students. Some go into the examination hall with questions already in their minds. So when they get into the questions are in front of them, they narrate what they must have studied which relates with what had been asked. Others are versed with certain topics but do not give out what they had been asked" With these insights, some of the parents and the students were nodding their heads in approval and as sign of acknowledgement of the fact that the message had been sent home.

"Did the pupils give the origin of cholera?" She asked and there was a big "yes" that thundered from the hall through the campus.

"Did they say some of the causes of cholera?" She asked again and they replied in the affirmative.

"Did the pupil say some of the ways through which cholera can be prevented?" Mme Ntabe Nnambi asked again.

"Yes," the audience replied.

"Did they answer the question as to what cholera is?" She inquired further and the answer was in the negative.

As Mme Ntabe Nnambi was about to conclude her presentation, Mbanwei shouted from behind. "I got it. I got it." Every one turned to look at what was going on. At that point in time. Mr. Zibi the discipline came and took down Mbanwei's name and took him outside. It was after the meeting that the parents explained to him that Mbanwei had been having serious academic problems and that was why he was excited with the educative talk.

In August that same year when the results were released, Mbanwei had eight papers. Two years later, he succeeded in the G.C.E Advanced Level with five papers. He was the first student ever admitted into the University Teaching Hospital in Yaoundé from City Bilingual College.

Albert Samah

Story Seven

Animal Palaver

Once upon a time, wildlife and domestic animals

had a fierce quarrel. Wildlife animals like lions, tigers, elephants, monkeys accused domestic animals especially cats and dogs for being traitors. They said these domestic animals were sell outs who had betrayed the cause of the animal kingdom.

They pointed that these so called domestic pets were once staunch members and supporters of the animal kingdom but are no longer worthy of the name animal because they left and joined mankind who carried and continues to carry wicked activities towards animals. The wildlife animals complained that these pets live in houses constructed by humans, eat food prepared and provided by humans and protect mankind. Wildlife also complained that these domestic animals have become intimate friends with mankind. During one of the quarrels between these brand of animals which took place around the Limbe Wildlife Centre, they both voiced out their grievances and positions.

"What should we have done? When mankind first took on our ancestors, they were kids. They could not protect themselves," Dog justified.

"Yes, but amongst your ancestors, they were grownups. They should have fought back. By then mankind hadn't modern weapons" Chimpanzee argued.

"Who said our ancestors did not make any attempt? Do you know how many human beings dogs, cats, goats and other animals wounded when their siblings were captured by mankind?" Dog barked out.

"Let's keep history aside. What we Wildlife are saying is that those siblings captured by mankind have been brainwashed. They did not fight back. As their descendants, you have joined in the process and every day you are being brainwashed. What is annoying is the fact that you are doing nothing about it," Tiger joined in.

"But you also have your species living in Zoos and Wild life Parks. Go to Limbe Wildlife Centre, to Waza National Park, to Mvog Beti Zoo and you will find Wildlife living happily and comfortably." Cat mewed sharply.

"What do you want them to do? They are protected within electric fences that can get them electrocuted if they ever attempt escaping. But you, especially you cats and dogs, move freely with mankind, carry him on your backs, eat his food, play with him and sometimes you even sleep with him on the same bed." Zebra said as he turned his neck.

Albert Samah

"Don't be ridiculous you Wildlife Animals. Don't you have your fellow brothers and sisters living in wild life centres and eating food prepared by human beings?" Speaking on behalf of the domestic animals, Dog accused with a loud bark.

"That is because they have no choice. To survive, they have to eat food prepared by mankind." Leopard reiterated.

"Why can't they go on hunger strike? Cat mewed.

"You should be comprehensive with mankind. When you say mankind is wicked and bad it is as though the entire mankind is bad. Those of us that are closer to humans have come to realize that some of them are very understanding. They take care of us and see into it that our progeny as well as yours is not wiped out by those who have no pity and interest for animals. Health wise, we have veterinary centres with doctors who are specialized for our welfare. In those centres, we are vaccinated free of charge. Free of charge in the sense that the services are paid by those who keep us in their houses." Goat highlighted.

"That is why we say you have been brainwashed. I am the king of the forest, I can never be friendly to mankind no matter what. I know this is the hypocrisy of mankind meant to deceive us and make us docile. Mankind is a liar," Lion roared.

"As I was saying, not all human beings are bad. Do you know there are some humans who will never eat our flesh? ...what do they call them again...yes vegetarians," Goat spoke.

"Yes, they will not eat those of you domestic animals like cat, dogs who have been brainwashed to the highest level," Lion roared sarcastically.

"No, what I mean is that they are human beings called vegetarians who will never eat the flesh of any animal."

"That is what I heard, but I am yet to believe that," Leopard said.

"As I was saying, some of them are truly friendly even to you Wildlife. That is why they have constructed Wildlife Centers so that those of you who are caught by some uncivilized men can be kept in and protected. Some of them have very good school programs which are organized to see that even if you die you will have someone to maintain your lineage. They call it in their language wildlife for survival. Do you know that some human beings have been sent to prison because they killed some of your species? I mean Wildlife," Cat mewed.

"Are you really certain of that?" Chimpanzee asked.

"Of course I am. There are natural and international laws meant to protect Wildlife. Animals like lion, chimpanzee and many others are highly protected." Dog informed them with a friendly bark.

"Yes, it sounds somehow absurd but it's true. There are nature, environment and earth clubs in schools campaigning amongst young people so that they can grow with an environment friendly attitude. By so doing, they will protect you and your offspring. This will also ensure that you and your offspring have food to live on," Cow added.

"That can be interesting," Zebra said.

"I hope it's not a trick to get us weak and finally make all of us become subservient like you domestic animals." Tortoise said.

"No, I think mankind has discovered that plants, animals and mankind form what is called the ecosystem. For him to survive, he needs us not just for food, but to keep this ecosystem together. He needs us; I mean both domestic and wildlife animals for survival. If he destroys all of us, it will have an adverse effect on his descendants," Camel said.

"Do human beings care about succeeding generations?" Zebra asked again.

"Some do. The enlightened ones do. As I was saying, mankind needs us and we also need him. We need him because only he can carry out research to see that we are protected from diseases and the changing climate."

"That is interesting but we must be very wise and careful" Porcupine said.

"I am not saying that we should not be careful with mankind. Like I said before, there are some of them who will not spare if they have an opportunity to exterminate us. These are the uncivilized ones. But others will go as far as organizing a funeral service if any one of us is killed. I mean both wildlife and domestic animals."

Although wild animals were still angry both with mankind and domestic animals, they knew within themselves that there is a cross section of mankind that has their interest at heart. They also knew that this cross section of mankind will do everything to see that they are protected and that they will have a progeny. This gave them some comfort.

The End

Story Eight

The Tests of Life

Thomas could not have been naive to give his hard-earned and life savings to any of his children without ensuring that they were qualified to handle the responsibilities that go with managing wealth. His four sons (Peter, John, Obina, Emeka) all had dreams of one day becoming the Chief Executive Officer of one of the biggest oil companies in the Gulf of Guinea.

That evening as they had dinner, Thomas expressed his appreciation for the manner in which Emeka handled the most recent deal struck with the Pakistani Oil Company. There was silence for close to five minutes after the deal was mentioned. Thomas could read envy, bitterness and jealousy on the faces of his other ambitious sons. He was not

Albert Samah

surprised with this for he had sought for an appropriate medium to address issues relating to this.

"I will not be the one to bring up this issue, there must be a clue," he told himself.

The plates and the spoons rang in the midst of the dead silence. Apologies of table manners ensued but no pleasantries or gossips as usual. After what seemed to be more than eternity, John broke the silence.

"Dad, it has always been my wish to handle the petrol company of this empire," Peter and Obina shrugged. An atmosphere of frustration slipped through their minds. By implication, John was already requesting to inherit this sector of the business when Dad would be no more. From every indication, Dad himself wishes Emeka handles it. These thoughts disjointedly assembled over the minds of Peter and Obina. But they held their patience and peace for their father had not openly made mention as to who was to handle and if possible inherit the most lucrative part of the business empire.

What will their father say? They all waited for his reply. In such scenario Thomas would simply leave the scene and walk into his bedroom. Sometimes he would simply take his wife out of the neighborhood for a ride. But this day, he decided to handle it.

"You will all have what you desire and ask for," he said stressing the last syllable of each word.

"It's not fair Dad and you know it. How could you say that when John is already requesting to own the entire business?" Peter retorted.

"Dad, how could you accept such a request?" Obina asked as he pushed away the plate of *Bongo* soup and *de maniock*.

"You know the two of us have not made any request." He added referring to Peter and himself.

"I have not given anything to anyone," Thomas protested authoritatively.

"But Dad, you just said we will have what we have asked for" Peter reminded him.

"Well, this is simply because you boys were not courteous and respectful enough to know that when an elderly person is speaking, you do not have to cut in. Else you should have gotten what I meant by that," Thomas said calmly. With this latest revelation, the four boys remained calm, waiting for whatever will come this time around.

Then, Thomas continued, "Each and every one will get what he wants and even much more but this will depend on the results of your various tests."

"Tests?" Peter and Obina asked while John looked at his father in bewilderment

"Yes, test. I mean every word of it," Thomas replied as he fought with the last slice of smoked meat remaining in his plate.

"Dad who is going to administer the test for us? Will you do it yourself or ask for one of your business partners to do it," Peter asked.

"All I know is that all tests relating to management or administration are the same," Peter boastfully acknowledged.

"I can still recall when last I failed a test. That was way back in primary school. Till I got my Masters in Business Administration, I knew that to pass a test, be it an end-of-course test or final examination, there are only one or two tricks. To begin, immediately a teacher gives a lesson, study that lesson within six hours. It sticks forever in your mind. After this, try to come out with many questions as possible relating to that lesson. When next you meet the same teacher, ask him the questions you must have established. Present to the teacher the most difficult ones. When he answers them, know that you have proposed the questions to be administered. In some cases, you possibly

Albert Samah

must have got more than half of the questions before the test," John reminisced and counseled as though he was insinuating that his brothers should go back to school.

"I can recall when I began having my best marks in school. This was when I discovered the need of establishing a study time table," Peter said to prove his own worth.

When the four young men realized they had been carried away with much of themselves and had moved away from their father who ought to be the center of the discussion, they became remorsefully quiet. Their discussion had given Thomas enough time to gather his thoughts and assemble them into wisdom. He then took a glass of water, swallowed it up in three gulps, picked up a tooth pick, cleared his throat and continued.

"Talking about academics and professionalism, you are all geniuses. This is why all of you have been successful in your past professional lives. But the test which is now set before you is quite another kind of test. It is the test of life. It is the test of values. It has little to do with academics or professionalism. To pass this test of life, you must earn the respect, trust and love of people especially to those you relate with in one way or the other. I know you were smart in school and even now you are smarter in your professional careers but know this: life will always throw things at you to test you."

He took a deep breath and after looking around he continued:

"Your promotion from one level of life to another will depend on the decisions and choices you make when life throws things at you. It will also depend whether you succeed or fail in the tests of life. Whenever you succeed in any of these tests, you are automatically promoted by society. It is from this that you earn the respect and trust of others. People do not love, respect or honour you because you have all the money in the world but because you have conquered their hearts, won their love and earned their respect."

At this point, it was as though the silence had increased for none of them was prepared to miss any of these words of wisdom. One could hear the tic-tac of the clock in the dining room while out of the gate.

"Sometimes human beings can be so manipulative with their praises," he continued. "They do this because of what they want to get out of the one they flatter. But if you have not for once gained their respect, be sure that deep down in their hearts, you will have no place, no worth and no value. They might be afraid of you especially if you have power over their lives in certain areas but this does not mean they respect or honour you. When the opportunity shows up and power or money is suddenly taken away from you, they will prove to you that they have never trusted nor respected you in the first place." He took a glass of water, sipped and continued,

"Sons, in life, you will be tested. Let no one take your place because you fail one of these tests."

"How then will you test us Dad?"Peter asked after he realized that Thomas had been silent for about three quarters of a minute. Stepping on this question, Thomas replied with a little story:

"There once lived a great king in Njidom. His wealth, fame and power were felt across several kingdoms. When time came for him to select his heir, he was deeply disturbed. He was conscious of the fact that his wealth and fame could bring division amongst his children and the king makers. He thought that if he were to simply write a will and allow

Albert Samah

55

members of his cabinet to reveal it after his death, personal
interest especially amongst the cabinet members could cause
them to tamper with the will. He also thought that his
judgment and choice for an heir could be misleading. So one
day, he decided to administer several tests to his children. He
thought that from these tests, he and his subjects would be
able to determine the next king. By so doing the future king
would win the trust and respect of the people.

He took a decision to assemble his children every evening so
as to teach them the ways of his kingdom. Each day had its
lesson. There were teachings on humility, honesty,
reconciliation, peacemaking, peace-building, forgiveness,
time management, respect for elders, premarital relationships
and self control. Topics such as courage, determination,
perseverance and wisdom were not left out.

In order to evaluate the impact of the lessons, the
king appointed seven secret secretaries to take daily accounts
on the activities of his seven sons. They were to write down
everything the sons said and did, that is, their words, actions,
facial expression, intentions, motives and gestures. So it was
that whenever the king's kids met for their training, the king
will pick up their daily activities and review them secretly.
Those who passed their tests were not only given more
responsibilities but also some power, honour and respect.

In one of such trainings the King talked on leaders as
servants. He said every good leader must be humble and
serviceable. He must be ready to protect and save lives
because the power bestowed on every leader is sufficient to
command respect. After this training, the King decided to
administer a test to his sons.

He placed an old man in a forest a few kilometres from his
palace and sent his sons to pass through that forest to a

nearby kingdom. When the princes got to where the man was, the old man asked for help. They could have helped but they reminded themselves that they were from the royal family so could not descend that low. They could not see themselves sitting on the same horse with a commoner.

When they left, Epolle one of the sons, came back secretly and carried the old man. He passed the test and this was written in the king's daily record. The old man who received help from Epolle narrated the story to his wife and children and this spread to the entire kingdom. The next test came during the celebration of the King's 75th birthday. It coincided with the celebration of the 350th Anniversary of the Kingdom of Njidom. To make the celebrations befitting, the king decided to make them to be for a month. He invited kings with their queens, princes and princesses from other kingdoms.

The kings and the queens were lodged in special guest houses meant for people of their caliber while the visiting princes and princesses were sent to a section of the palace reserved for princes and princesses. As there was a lot of merry making and some amount of liberty, most of the princes and princesses indulged in all types of immoral acts. There was excessive drinking, smoking and sexual immorality. While this was going on, the seven secret secretaries were on duty. They registered the activities of the seven potential heirs. They did this throughout the entire celebrations. While others were fully engaged in these immoral acts, Epolle and Elangwe decided they would remain pure throughout the feast. Realizing this, their brothers encouraged princesses from the visiting kingdoms to seduce them.

After a great struggle, Elangwe ended up falling during the last days.

"Did Epolle hold on till the end?" Peter asked.

"On one occasion he got into his room and met one of the princesses completely naked,"

Thomas continued, "He ran out of his room and spent the rest of the night with one of the palace guards. This was also noted by the king's secretary in the King's register.

After the celebrations, the seven secret secretaries brought their reports before the king made changes accordingly. Epolle was given the responsibility, titles and privileges meant for the first born son though he was last amongst the King's sons. The kings's children were tested on forgiveness, courage and in several other areas based on their capacities. Before the king's death, Epolle had taken the position of the first born.

Before the king's death, he asked for the register to be brought and open before his children and cabinet members. It was no surprise to the King's sons, the members of the king's cabinet and even the subjects that Epolle was heir of the kingdom. He, like the others, was tried, tested and proven. Though he had failed in some areas, nevertheless he passed the tests of life. Epolle had earned the trust, love and respect of the people. They were willing, ready and happy to have him as their king.

When Thomas finished the story, he took a deep breath and sat quiet. While employing a toothpick to do justice to his teeth, there was silence for close to five minutes. Then Peter spoke,

"Dad why did you choose this story and where on earth did you get it from?"

"Where I got it is not important. What is important is the lesson behind it. You will all be tested with the tests of life. As a human being, I might make mistakes on how to apportion responsibilities, privileges and resources to each and every one of you. But know that your happiness, fulfillment and all you will ever be in this life and even in the life to come will not depend on how much you grab from this empire. But it will depend on whether you pass or fail the tests of life. True respect, honour, joy, happiness, peace of mind, fulfillment and prosperity only comes when you must have passed the tests of forgiveness, humility, love, serviceability, self control and much more. Sons, let no one take your places in life. Epolle took that of the first born of the king simply because the latter failed his tests. There is a place for everybody. No one can take your place except... I say except you fail the tests of life."

This story sank deep into the hearts of these four ambitious young men. They all made up their minds to do their best to pass whatever test was set before them by their father and society as a whole. This affected their relationships with their colleagues, friends and even subordinates. Their attitude towards people, power, positions, titles and popularity improved greatly. Thomas witnessed this positive change on a daily basis. He felt a sense of satisfaction. He was certain that even after his death, not only would the empire continue to grow, but also his children would live peacefully.

It was for this reason that he put in place a rotational inheritance system. By this, one of his sons was to control the key sectors of his empire for a period of three years. Thereafter, he was to hand it over to another until all of them had served as President of the empire. Part of the profits from the empire was distributed amongst the sons while the rest was set outside for the upkeep and growth of the empire.

Whenever Thomas' sons met in their annual family reunion with wives and children, they made sure that they recounted the story of the king and the tests he administered to his seven sons. This is how Thomas succeeded to transmit values to his descendants.

The End

Story Nine

*S*earching for Identities

*F*or over five hundred years the people of Bimbia

had mourned and wept for their sons and daughters. They were gathered, packaged and sailed across the Atlantic Ocean to the Americas where they worked as slaves. The Bimbia community had always felt that part of them was missing and that until the descendants of their ancestors who were carried away were brought home, that emptiness would always remain with them forever.

They therefore longed for the day when this part of their being would be reunited so that their completeness would be felt again. But five hundred years is a long time and even if their children were to ever return, they would certainly not

Albert Samah

aptly fit within the Bimbia cultural norms. Every right thinking being would have thought in this manner but this was not the case for attitude is in the pattern of the blood line.

It was in the early 2000s that the *returning-to-my-roots* phenomenon of daughters and sons of former slaves gained ground. Greatly influenced by black American stars like the television talk show icon Winfred Oprah who herself had mistakenly traced her origin to South Africa, many African Americans began tracing their identities to the different parches of land in this continent of great controversies: Africa.

When the first vague of Cam-Americans announced their home coming, it was a national issue, highly promoted by the media. Sons and daughters who had lived all their lives in the United States of America were coming to see the paths their ancestors trod before getting to the sea shores and to the Americas. This was on almost every press organ especially the state media organs. Their coming became the headline news on the national radio and television. Their arrival was scheduled for 4 p.m Central African Time. This was of course a salient issue for the press. It was mentioned in one of the private newspapers that the government intended to use this event to cleanse the nation's image abroad and also use these Americans as crusaders and promoters of Cameroon's progress in issues of human rights and democracy in the international community.

As the Minister of Communication drove from his Bastos neighbourhood through Rosa Parks Avenue, just a few metres from the America Embassy, he found a long line of Cameroonians waiting still to be attended to by the Immigration Department of this embassy. Some were applying for the Green Card, others for visas to go and meet loved ones while some were seeking for study visas thanks to the *docky* admission letters they had obtained through the help of their brothers residing in Bonamoussadi, the Yaoundé University Student Residential Area .

One thing was strong and certain on the Minister's mind: He knew deep within his being that these were young Cameroonians searching for an identity they could not easily find in their own home land. These tired and hopeless faces, carrying little bags hung on their chests and waists, reminded the Minister of the pictures he once saw on the lesson on slave trade he had studied in High School more than half a century earlier.

He quickly pushed away these thoughts, picked up the state owned bilingual daily and read an article on himself on the last press conference he gave on government's position on corruption and embezzlement.

By 3.55 p.m. it was announced that due to some technical errors, Boeing *6777-Palapala* would not be landing as expected. It would only arrive by 6:45 p.m. so one of the airport officials quickly gave a professional excuse and hung up the microphone.

In the midst of the smiles and jokes, one could notice the frustration and discouragement amongst the minister and his entourage. With this announcement, the traditional dance groups that had accompanied the traditional rulers and elite from the South West Region played and danced even harder. It was as though their songs and dance were going to provoke the plane to come earlier than the time announced. Opposite the Minister and his entourage were a group of family members who had come to bid farewell to their

Albert Samah

fortunate children, brothers, sisters, husbands and wives leaving for the United States of America.

Amongst these potential *bush fallers* was Musa Philip. After his graduation from the University Teaching Hospital Yaoundé, he had practiced as a medic in Bali, Fundong, Bafut and Ndop. He considered himself very fortunate when this opportunity came his way. He was going to meet thirty of his mates of the fortieth batch of the University Teaching Hospital who had left to start life in the United States. They had all left within the space of ten years after their graduation to where they believed the quality of their pay package would match the quality of their services.

Tambu Joseph on his part graduated from the Higher Teacher Training College (Ecole Normal) Yaoundé. Upon graduation as the forty- third batch in Economics, he was sent to teach English Language in C.E.S de Maroua. He lived for three years dabbling on a field which was quite different from what he studied in the training college and wondering if his salary the state had accumulated for over three years- would ever come. Now that the *gros lot (accrued salary arrears)* was out and he could collect his monthly salary, he could pay the man who had arranged for his *docky* to travel and could also secure his air ticket for the US. As he sat waiting for the check in, he took a deep breath and congratulated himself on the decision he had made with his monthly salary. A quarter of his income would go to the principal of the school he was posted to teach while the rest would go to his account in Biabia Bank. From this account he would be able to issue a cheque to Chief Ako to refund part of the loan he taken to make his way into the Higher Teacher Training College.

Sitting adjacent Tambu was Sidney and Joseph. They were also leaving for the United States. Looking on their faces, one would conclude that Sidney was one of the most fortunate human beings in this part of the world. She was one of the two Cameroonians who had won the American DV after trying for ten times.

With a second class upper in Journalism and Mass Communication from the University of Buea, she had tried desperately in vain to work with CRTV, the state owned television and radio. Even though she got a job with several private media houses, it was only to keep her busy and to help her build good curriculum vitae for better days ahead. When she received a letter from the United States Embassy in Cameroon informing her that she had won the U.S Diversity Lottery her happiness was still incomplete.

With her financial status, getting the necessary papers required by the US Embassy within the recorded time was near to impossibility. Her father's meagre salary and savings as a mission primary school teacher would never help the situation. She understood all of this. What she needed was a miracle of some kind. Her mother unlike her father was a woman who knew how to make things happen. Within record time, she arranged for an impromptu wedding with Sidney the son of her younger sister. Margaret her younger sister was the type that would never let opportunities pass by without reaping any kind of benefit. She had insisted on the wedding when her elder sister asked for a loan for Sidney's project to travel. She was the one who paid for the wedding arrangements, the medical checkups, the passports, the visa fee and the flight tickets.

Both groups had one thing in common: They were both waiting and hoping. Those leaving for the US were waiting

Albert Samah

for the check in which had been delayed by the minister's unexpected stay at the airport. They kept thinking and hoping that the new world ahead of them would bring the happiness that the Western media projects. On the other side of the airport was the minister and his entourage waiting and hoping. Waiting impatiently that this new phenomenon of home coming would bring positive changes to the political landscape of the country. As both groups wondered in hopes, Boeing *6777-Palapala* scratched its wheel on the Nsamalen International Airport.

Folding up his *gandura*, the minster stood up as he moved towards the lane to greet the head of Cam-American delegation. Dressed in an Indomitable Lions' jersey carrying the name Eto'o, Mr. Michael immediately turned on a smile as he noticed the presence of the minister by the size of his clothes. With a firm grip and wide open arms, Michael embraced the minister and put his hand on his shoulders as he introduced the rest of his delegation. Before presenting the short speech prepared for this new breed of Cameroonians, one of the Cam-Americans complainted that the government of Cameroon did not make provision for their complete transportation and lodging.

As the minister's speech came closer to an end, a member of the entourage whispered to one of his colleagues,
"There is no way on earth that one could say these are not Cameroonians."
"What makes you so certain? Have you forgotten that there was a controversy as to Oprah Winfred's origin?" His colleague whispered back.
"These Americans have the Cameroonian blood and mentality in them."
"How?"

"Hardly have they arrived, I heard one complaining what the government did not do for them. What have they done for Cameroonians for God's sake?"

"I hope they are not just Americans coming to visit Cameroon as tourists"

Picking up their luggage, those traveling to the United States queued up as their names were distinctly stressed out by the airport official for the first check in. Tambu and three others who had made fake papers moved into the cabin for the check up while their loved ones stood outside waiting and praying that their last hope would not be dashed away by the professionalism of a single airport official. Three of Tambu's friends had already been checked including himself. It was at that point that there was power failure making the Nsimalen airport completely dark.

"This is a sign of ill luck" A member of the Cam-American delegation commented.

"I told you that these people are our children," One of the Chiefs from the South West Region said happily.

"He could sense evil by reading events. If it were the days of my ancestors, we could have taken him even against his wish and make him chief priest."

It was after thirty minutes that the American Company, A.E.S Sonel, decided to bring back life to the airport. When the lights came back, there were sobs, weeping and mourning in a cross section of the airport. Three of the four young men with the *dockies (fake documents) were* discovered and their passports seized. One through some kind of luck had succeeded to make his way through.

The *ducky* men who had come to collect the rest of the money for the deal had quietly disappeared in their Cherokee

Albert Samah

Jeep which was parked a few metres from the airport gate. The three young men whose passports were seized including Tambu joined the delegation that had come to receive their brothers from America who had also come to look for their identity. As they drove through the forest of the Nsamalen International Airport, these three young men wondered where their identities and allegiances really were. A similar thought flashed through the minds of the Americans who had come to look for their identities and roots in Cameroon.

The End

Story Ten

The Missing Talent

It was 5:30 P.M Central African Time when Nwanchan packed the jeep beside a pile of wood adjacent one of the mud huts in Njimben. It was a long but interesting journey. There was little interference and argument from Susan on his speed level. He had gone up to 170 Km an hour. The kids themselves had fallen asleep immediately they had crossed Obala and got up only in Makenene. After the stop, they had fallen asleep again for almost all the journey.

Nwanchan felt a thought of satisfaction and pride running down his spinal cord as he pulled the handbrake of the car.

Albert Samah

He was certainly the first to bring a vehicle of this calibre to Njimben. Children with muddy bodies lined up to get a closer look of their faces from the glittering of this black painted American jeep. The rays of the retiring sun deflected their half miserable faces on the bonnet of the car. Then the greetings ensued from every corner, greetings accompanied with expectations of a handshake of bread and other goodies from the city.

Then the kids jumped out of the car, stretched themselves with airs of some American movie super star, wondering how on earth people could live in such a far corner of the earth and still have smiles on their faces. As they accepted the greetings, they watched carefully so that the warm embrace from the women and children and the odour coming from their old clothes do not leave behind a remarkable stain on their city dress.

Ndaya stood motionless for close to five minutes while his imagination administered a series of questions without attempting any answer. Starring at the half finished basket Manyi almost buried with her large bare feet when she heard the sound of the vehicle, he marveled at the magic that could weave the backs of the bamboo horizontally and vertically.

"Manyi is not different from the cane chairs weavers," Ndaya thought. His passion to know how the bamboo backs intermingle horizontally and vertically made him spend most of his playing moments during the summer holidays watching how baskets were being made.

Once in Yaoundé, the passion almost vanished until his mother accidentally drove past the Olezoa neighborhood. With diverse types of wood works, cane chairs and tables luxuriously exhibited along the main streets, Ndaya's curiosity on arts and wood work was immediately rekindled. He happened to have seen a sample of the cane chairs in one of the sitting rooms in the residence of the Nigerian Consulate in the Bastos neighborhood when Mr. Nwanchan and his entire family were invited for a party.

Curiosity flamed within his soul. Sometimes when his pocket allowance got finished, Ndaya would dash unnoticed from home, crossing several neighborhoods, using numerous short cuts from their residential area in Damas heeding for Olezoa. For two to three hours, he would ask questions and watch how the canes were transformed into sofas, side stools, tables and cupboards. This new phenomenon went on for close to two years unnoticed until that fateful day. As he crossed over from Kinge's workshop to get a cab home, he bumped into his father's jeep.

For the first time in his life, Mr. Nwanchan mercilessly beat up his child in public, a thing he himself had never imagined could ever happen. This incident would mark a turning point in Mr. Nwanchan's family.

"I think you have over reacted," Mrs. Nwanchan complained.

"Do you really think so? I would not allow him drag my personality into that mud," Mr. Nwachan pointed out sharply.

"So you call that mud? What is wrong with just watching that activity? You forget too soon that your great grandfather was a sculptor who made masks for Obasinjong. This thing could be hereditary and..." Mrs. Nwanchan indicated as the slap from Mr. Nwanchan carried her to the floor.

"Never mention that in the presence of my children. Do you know how much I have worked to get away from that?" Mrs. Nwanchan was on the floor for close to twenty five minutes before being rushed to a nearby clinic.

Things could have been more horrific if Ndaya did not make it in the Advanced Level Examinations. He passed in History, French, and Literature in English with all Bs grades. The kind of university studies on which he could build his career watered down the new happiness that had germinated after the past months of mistrust in Mr. Nwanchan's family.

Mr. Nwanchan's dream of seeing his son study law in the University of Yaoundé II which will prepare him for entrance into the Advanced School of Administration and Magistracy popularly known in its French acronym as ENAM, collided with Ndaya's dream of studying theater arts and painting in the University of Yaoundé I.

Ndaya would have to pay the price for a dream he believed in. If it was really a dream then he would have to forfeit some, if not all of his privileges. Not just the privileges that an ordinary person enjoys to make it in life but that of being Mr. Nwanchan's son.

If his decision was ignorance messed up with stupidity and childishness, he would have to be humble enough to come to the realities of life and ask for forgiveness from his father before opportunities disappear.
A full academic year had come and gone with Ndaya not knowing exactly where his fate lay. He had rather indulged in painting, an art he had come to discover of late that he was gifted in.

Mrs. Nwanchan believed that the passions and skills lurking within his son where hereditary. Mr. Nwanchan's great grandfather himself was a great sculptor whose skills were employed to manufacture *Afoa Akum*, a mask that was stolen and carried abroad. Her own grandfather was apt in playing drums and composing songs. It was said that before Zintgraph ever visited Bali, he entertained the Fon of Bali. She had seen Ndaya demonstrate skills in singing, carving and painting. She believed that the skills were inherited and could be nurtured, and groomed into a more useful treasure. This explains why she covertly sympathized with Ndaya's choice of studying arts in the university.

The relationship with her husband had moved from emotional, to intellectual and was at a level of mistrust, complaints and trap setting. Even when discussions surfaced time and again, they were usually formal with little or no empathy.

The registration date for the new academic year was gradually coming to the end and Mr. Nwanchan was still steadfast on his position. It was either Ndaya studied law and he took full responsibility for his studies or he studied whatever he deemed necessary and got nothing from him. Mr. Nwanchan insisted that he had worked hard to build political and business networks that could enable his son get into one of the most prestigious professional schools in the country.

He swore that he would never be part of that conspiracy that would cause his son to be at the mercy of tourists. He insisted his son's salary would not come from the musical preferences of the masses and tourists.

"The time has come for me to take a stand," Mrs. Nwanchan told herself. She got Ndaya registered in the University of Yaoundé 1. This action was more or less signing in for a divorce. Mr. Nwanchan began slashing the feeding and upkeep allowances into four with the intention

Albert Samah

that this would stop Mrs. Nwanchan from pursuing her new venture. When it did not succeed, he virtually stopped giving any allowances.

By the second year in the university, Ndaya was practically sponsoring himself. However, by declining from taking responsibility for Ndaya's education, health and feeding, Mr. Nwanchan gave Ndaya the opportunity to discover more of his gifts and talents. Mr. Nwanchan's punitive measures to send Ndaya packing into the boys' quarters were rather an opportunity for him to maximize his potentials. His new room was nothing short of a workshop and an exhibition centre. Portraits of people of all works of life, sculptures of different animals, plants and people were displayed therein. Just beside his two inch plank bed was a drawer with files of songs which he had composed, some of which he sang during weddings, birthday parties and other cultural events. His passion for arts and craft made him to sometime work for several hours and in most cases very late into the night.

"What could have been the cause of this illness?" Mrs. Nwanchan pondered as she sat opposite Ndaya, watching him as he battled to keep his breath going. Ndaya had been in the hospital for six weeks now and Mr. Nwanchan's visit to him was still expensive to come by. From when he fell ill Mrs. Nwanchan had endeavoured on putting one and two together to buy the medication prescribed by the doctor. But getting Ndaya to the Douala Referral Hospital for a surgery as prescribed by Dr. Dauda Mathew was what she could not think of handling all by herself. All her savings in the Azire Cooperative Union and the other two thrift schemes popularly referred to as *Njangi* groups which she was faithfully contributing, could not save her from this predicament.

Her last hope was that by seeing Ndaya's medical report, Mr. Nwanchan's heart would be softened. But this device did not bear the expected fruits because Mr. Nwanchan kept insisting that Ndaya had to accept changing his career option before he could step in with the necessary finance for the surgery. It was only when an emergency family meeting championed by Mrs. Nwanchan was held in Mr. Nwanchan's residence that Mr. Nwanchan compromised his position and accepted to fly Ndaya to Douala the following day. But before the necessary arrangements were made for the flight, Ndaya had crossed over the shores of life.

Ndaya's death was the divorce letter that formally separated Mr. Nwanchan and his wife. Despite several meetings organized by family members and friends who acted as third parties, the key that sealed Mrs. Nwanchan's heart from ever letting her husband come in was locked with the burial of Ndaya. It was of no use trying. She packed her belongings and left.

Although she left Mr. Nwanchan, Ndaya would never leave her presence. She could feel him several months even after the burial. She could hear him in his songs, see him in his paintings especially the portrait he made of her. She secured a room in her new premises where Ndaya's works were displayed exactly as they were in his room when he was alive.

Two years after the death of Ndaya, she was yet to come to terms with life. She was about turning a new page by letting Elangwe Johnson come into her life. Ever since Elangwe returned from the United States after having lived there for close to fifteen years, he had shown keen interest in   Mrs. Nwanchan. On her part, Mrs. Nwanchan had resisted on the grounds that she was still someone's wife, an excuse she

Albert Samah

gave to let her heart completely heal and to find out more on the character of this *bush faller*.

It was only when she had made up her mind to give in to Elangwe that an international exhibition for crafts and paintings was launched, organized by several countries to be hosted in *Africa in miniature*, Cameroon. This exhibition was to bring in participants from almost every country on the face of the earth. To honour the promise she made on Ndaya's dying bed, Mrs. Nwanchan resolved that before she opened up in response to Elangwe's advances she must exhibit Ndaya's works to the general public. She believed she would have peace and rest in her soul if her son's dying wishes were respected.

So Mrs. Nwanchan signed up for a stand with the Ministry of Arts and Culture of the Republic of Cameroon. Within the space of a week, three quarters of Ndaya's works had been bought with some selling for up to two million CFA francs. By the time the exhibition was over, she had sold articles worth close to twenty three million CFA Francs.

This money was immediately invested into the construction of a centre to train young artists, musicians, sculptors, painters and writers. It was during the inauguration ceremony of the Ndaya's Foundation that Mr. Nwanchan and his wife finally reconciled. Their broken home and marriage was once more restored. Within the space of three years the Ndaya Foundation had established three hundred young people in the field of painting, carving, weaving and writing.

Glossary

Docky: Fake documents

Gros lots: Accrued salary arrears

Cha'avum: Locally fabricated guns

Chef du quartier: Quarter head

Baba: witch doctor

Bush faller: One who has traveled or lived abroad

Afoa Akum: Traditional masquerade

Pichichi: Spanish word which means champion

Achu and yellow soup: traditional meal from the North West Region of Cameroon.

Bongo Soup and Baton de manioc: Traditional meal from the Litoral Region of Cameroon.

Obasinjong: Masquerade

Njangi: Thrift schemes

Albert Samah

THE ULTIMATE SEARCH: PERSONAL WORD

Every human person, of every sex and of every status was consciously created with specific gifts, talents, potentials and knowhow for a specific reason best known to the Creator. These potentials and purposes have been consciously and unconsciously misunderstood, misapplied, distorted, and trampled upon by wrong ideas, philosophies, and decisions emanating from the corruption of the human heart. This is the cause of fear, failure, low self esteem and hopelessness, which in most cases is demonstrated in acts like murder, jealousy, bitterness, alcoholism, adultery, fornication, stealing, conflict, genocide and terrorism.

Within each and every human person, is that deep desire to be free, to be happy, to be successful, to be great and to be relevant. Knowingly or unknowingly this search has most often been sought in areas and in those very things that trap and imprison the human soul of its greatest longing; the desire to be totally free, happy and be in the perpetual state of peace.

Where gifts and talents have been identified, they have most often been used for personal and sometimes egocentric purposes without taking into consideration the giver of these gifts or the programmes for which these gifts, talents and skills were made available. Sometimes greatness is achieved through the wrong paths which explains the inner emptiness that comes along with certain achievements and success

Deep in the Creator's heart is this desire to see mankind totally liberated. It is His wish to see His creatures live in total freedom, joy and fulfillment. It is His preoccupation to

Weeping Environment

see His creatures live out their best within the framework of the reasons and programs for which they were created. It is His concern that His creatures deepen their knowledge of Him into a new and living relationship that will reconcile them with Him. The image of God in every human person is a springboard and a magnate through which mankind can reconnect to His creator. His word is then made available to fertilize every dream, talent, skill and potential that has been buried through fear, racism, ethnicity, mediocrity, triviality, wrong decisions and hatred. This new relationship can open individuals into a new world of faith, possibilities hope, peace, righteousness, integrity, joy and fulfillment as they fulfill their dreams and look forward to eternal bliss. It is only through this that mankind can talk of true success!

Albert Samah

Made in the USA
Middletown, DE
18 January 2024